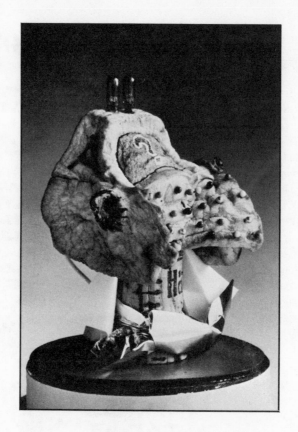

Introducing MR. CHIPS, the Real Apple Computer. Leon Bishop,
Ann Bishop's husband, designed and carved Mr. Chips,
combining new hardware with the old American folk art of
apple carving. Mr. Chips may be the only real "apple" computer in the world.

HELLO, MR. CHIPS!

Computer Jokes & Riddles

by **ANN BISHOP**

drawings by Jerry Warshaw

LODESTAR BOOKS

E.P. Dutton   New York

HELLO, MR. CHIPS!
HELLO, MR. CHIPS!
HELLO, MR. CHIPS!
HELLO, MR. CHIPS!
HELLO, MR. CHIPS!
HELLO, MR. CHIPS!
HELLO, MR. CHIPS!
HELLO, MR. CHIPS!

Library of Congress Cataloging in Publication Data
Bishop, Ann.
  Hello, Mr. Chips!

  Summary: A collection of riddles involving computers.
    1. Computers—Anecdotes, facetiae, satire, etc. 2. Riddles. [1. Computers—Anecdotes, facetiae, satire, etc. 2. Riddles]
I. Warshaw, Jerry, ill. II. Title.
PN6231.E4B5 1982   818.′5402   81-17105
ISBN 0-525-66775-X   AACR2
ISBN 0-525-66782-2 (pbk.)
Editor: Virginia Buckley

Published in the United States by E. P. Dutton, Inc., 2 Park Avenue, New York, N.Y. 10016.

Printed in the U.S.A.
10 9 8 7 6 5 4 3

I would like to acknowledge, with thanks,
the witty contributions of my friends—
Geoffrey Garvey
Barbara Thompson and
Harold Bordwell

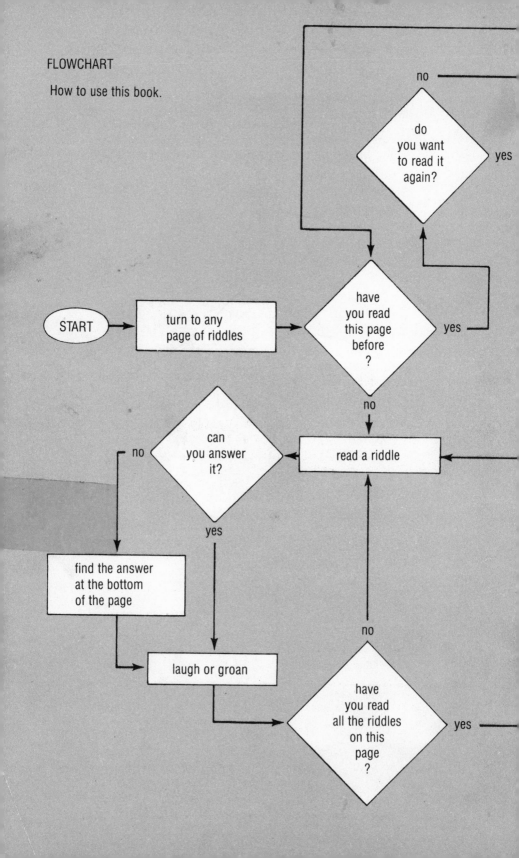

FLOWCHART

How to use this book.

do you want to read it again? — no / yes

START → turn to any page of riddles → have you read this page before ? — yes / no

can you answer it? — no / yes

read a riddle

find the answer at the bottom of the page

laugh or groan

have you read all the riddles on this page ? — no / yes

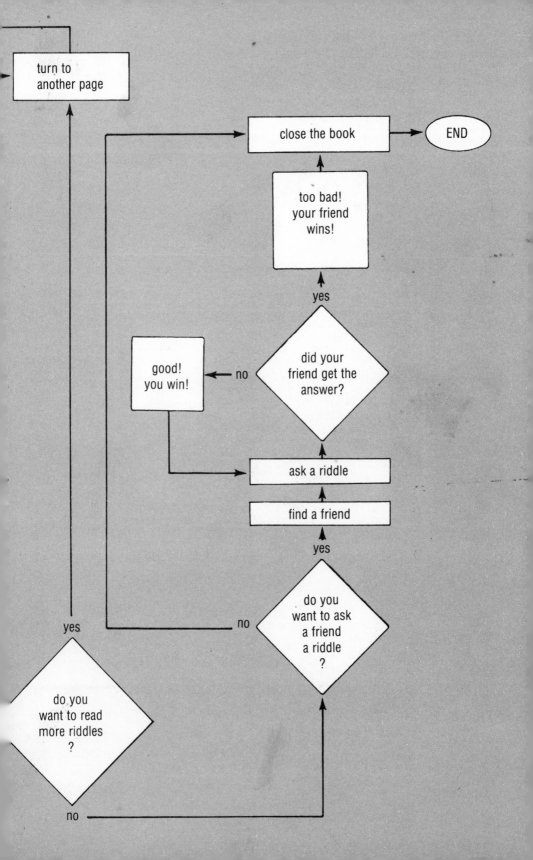

5 REM SOMETHING OLD, SOMETHING NEW

WHAT'S BLACK AND WHITE AND RED ALL OVER?

WHY DID THE COMPUTER CROSS THE ROAD?

A printout from Russia.

It had the chicken's number.

10 REM COMPUTERS AND THEIR HUMANS

DO COMPUTERS LIKE HUMAN BEINGS?

WHICH IS FASTER, A COMPUTER OR A HUMAN BEING?

Yes—human beings turn them on.

Wait—let me think about that one.

WHAT'S A PROGRAMMER?

WHICH WAY DID THE PROGRAMMER GO?

WHAT DO PROGRAMMERS HAVE IN COMMON WITH SPIES?

WHAT DO YOU CALL AN AGING PROGRAMMER?

HOW DO YOU MAKE A COMPUTER LAUGH?

A human who gives a computer a chance to display all its error messages.

He went data way.

They both write in code.

An old softie.

Tell it a programmer joke.

WHAT DID THE SYSTEMS ENGINEER SAY TO THE NOISY APPLE?

WHY DID ITS HUMAN TAKE THE COMPUTER FOR A WALK EVERY DAY?

WHAT WAS THE HUMAN PLAYING THAT SENT ITS PET TO THE VET?

If you're not quiet, I'll take a byte out of you.

The computer was a Pet.

Loop-the-loop.

WHY IS THE NEWEST COMPUTER ALMOST HUMAN?

CAN COMPUTERS RUN AWAY FROM HOME?

WHAT SHOULD YOU DO WITH A COMPUTER THAT'S A YEAR OLD?

When it makes a mistake, it can put the blame on another computer.

Not unless someone plugs them in.

Wish it a happy birthday.

16 REM DAFFINITIONS

MICROCOMPUTER:	Patrocomputer's brother.
MINICOMPUTER:	Patrocomputer and Microcomputer's sister.
TERMINAL GLARE:	A look that kills.
INPUT:	A short stroke that sinks a golf ball in the cup.
OUTPUT:	What you do to the cat before you go to bed.

20 REM COMPUTERS—A FEW OF THEIR FAVORITE THINGS

WHAT'S A COMPUTER'S FAVORITE SONG?

WHAT'S A COMPUTER'S FAVORITE ELLA FITZGERALD NUMBER?

WHAT'S A TEXAS COMPUTER'S FAVORITE SONG?

WHO'S A COMPUTER'S FAVORITE ITALIAN FILM STAR?

WHAT'S A COMPUTER'S FAVORITE SPORT?

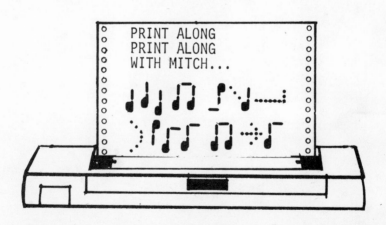

"Thanks for the Memory."

"A-Diskette, A-Daskette."

"Catalog, Little Dogie."

Gina Lollodigita.

Running.

WHAT'S A COMPUTER'S FAVORITE MOUNTAIN?

WHAT'S A COMPUTER'S FAVORITE RIDE AT AN AMUSEMENT PARK?

WHAT'S A COMPUTER'S FAVORITE CHRISTMAS CAROL?

WHAT'S A COMPUTER'S FAVORITE PRECISION DANCE TEAM?

Pike's Peek.

Loop-the-loop.

"Array in a Manger."

The Diskettes.

25 REM YOU AND YOUR COMPUTER

WHAT HAPPENS IF YOU HIT YOUR COMPUTER TOO HARD?

WHAT DO YOU GET IF YOU'RE NOT GOOD TO YOUR APPLE?

WHEN YOUR COMPUTER IGNORES YOU, HOW DO YOU GET ITS ATTENTION?

WHAT SHOULD YOU DO IF YOU DROP YOUR COMPUTER?

It goes down for the count.

A crab apple.

Poke it.

Let the chips fall where they may.

WHAT SHOULD YOU DO IF YOU GET PEANUT BUTTER ON YOUR FLOPPY?

WHEN IS A COMPUTER MOST UNGRATEFUL?

HOW DO YOU KNOW THAT COMPUTERS ARE FEMALE?

SHOULD YOU BE AFRAID OF A COMPUTERIZED DOG?

HOW DO YOU KNOW WHEN YOUR COMPUTER IS ANGRY?

Diskard it.

When it bytes the hand that feeds it.

They're compu*thers*, not compu*this*.

No. Its bark is worse than its byte.

It'll have a chip on its shoulder.

WHY IS IT A GOOD IDEA TO DO YOUR TAXES ON A COMPUTER?

HOW DO YOU TELEPHONE FROM A COMPUTER?

WHAT DO YOU CALL THE FASTEST COMPUTER IN THE WORLD?

Because you get a diskount.

It's easy. When you press the RETURN key on a computer, you don't get any money back.

A presto digitator.

30 REM TOM SWIFT
IN THE COMPUTER ROOM

"THIS COMPUTER WORKS WITH THE SPEED OF LIGHT," TOM SAID SWIFTLY.

"MY DEAR AUNT SALLY, YOU ALWAYS HAVE PRECEDENCE," TOM SAID CALCULATINGLY.

"THIS COMPUTER DOESN'T DISPLAY CAPITAL LETTERS,' TOM SAID SHIFTLESSLY.

"I CAN'T GET OUT OF THIS LOOP," TOM SAID ENDLESSLY.

35 REM YOUR COMPUTER IN SICKNESS AND IN HEALTH

WHAT DO YOU GIVE A SICK COMPUTER?

WHAT DID THE COMPUTER SAY ABOUT ITS ILLNESS WHEN IT GOT BETTER?

HOW DOES A COMPUTER DIE?

WHAT HAPPENED TO THE OLD COMPUTER?

Digitalis.

"Boy, that really knocked me for a loop."

It comes down with a terminal illness.

It fell to bits.

WHAT DID THE MOTHER COMPUTER SAY TO HER
SICK BABY?

WHY WAS THE COMPUTER CRANKY?

WHAT'S A SURE SIGN OF OLD AGE IN A COMPUTER?

WHAT'S A COMPUTER'S MOST COMMON DENTAL PROBLEM?

WHAT BACK PROBLEM DO COMPUTERS HAVE?

"Never mind, dear. We'll soon have those nasty bugs out of your system."

It was out of sorts.

Loss of memory.

Malocclusion, or overbyte.

Slipped disks.

HOW DOES A COMPUTER FEEL WHEN IT'S UP?

HOW DOES A COMPUTER FEEL WHEN IT'S DOWN?

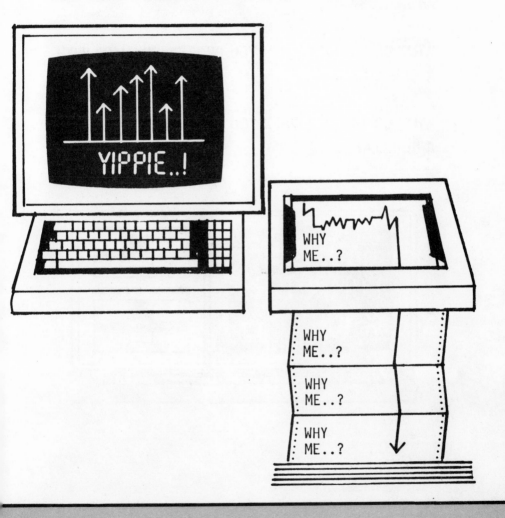

Chipper.

Diskonnected, diskontented, and diskgusted.

40 REM CROSSHATCHING

WHAT DO YOU GET WHEN YOU CROSS MINNEHAHA WITH AN ABACUS?

WHAT DO YOU GET WHEN YOU CROSS MINNEHAHA WITH A COMPUTER?

WHAT DO YOU GET WHEN YOU CROSS A COMPUTER WITH A GORILLA?

A minnecomputer.

A very small computer that gives you funny answers.

A hairy reasoner.

45 REM FEEDING YOUR COMPUTER

WHAT DO COMPUTERS EAT?

HOW DO COMPUTERS COOK?

HOW DO THEY CHOOSE THEIR MEALS?

A bit of almost anything.

In microwave ovens.

From menus, of course.

WHAT'S THEIR FAVORITE FOOD?

WHAT'S THEIR FAVORITE FUN FOOD?

DO COMPUTERS HAVE GOOD TABLE MANNERS?

Alphabit soup.

Silly corn chips.

Yes. They take very small bytes.

50 REM COMPUTERS AT WORK

HOW DOES A COMPUTER DO ITS JOB?

WHAT HAPPENED TO THE COMPUTER THAT TRIED OUT
FOR A MOVIE?

WHAT DO COMPUTER BEES DO?

Bit by bit.

It got a bit part.

They make honeywell.

WHAT NEW JOB DID THE COMPUTER GET?

WHERE ARE COMPUTER SOLDIERS STATIONED?

WHY DID THE COMPUTER THAT WORKED FOR THE SANITARY DISTRICT GET FIRED?

It posed for the centerfold in *Popular Mechanics*.

In a fortran.

Garbage in, garbage out.

WHAT DID THE COMPUTER SAY TO THE ADDING MACHINE?

WHAT DID THE COMPUTER SAY TO THE BANK TELLER?

WHY ISN'T THE COMPUTER WORKING?

"Anything you can do, I can do better!"

"You can count on me!"

The little person inside is taking a coffee break.

WILL COMPUTERS EVER DRIVE CARS?

WHAT KIND OF CAR WILL A COMPUTER DRIVE?

They will if they can pass the driver's license test.

A voltswagon.

55 REM KNOCK KNOCKS

KNOCK KNOCKS! KNOCK KNOCKS! KNOCK KNOCKS! KNOCK KNOCKS! KNOCK
NOCK KNOCKS! KNOCK KNOCKS! KNOCK KNOCKS! KNOCK KNOCKS! KN
S! KNOCK KNOCKS! KNOCK KNOCKS! KNOCK KNOCKS! KNOCK KNOCKS
NOCKS! KNOCK KNOCKS! KNOCK KNOCKS! KNOCK KNOCKS! KNOCK KN
CK KNOCKS! KNOCK KNOCKS! KNOCK KNOCKS! KNOCK KNOCKS! KNO

KNOCK KNOCK!

WHO'S THERE?

DIGITAL.

DIGITAL WHO?

DIGITAL YOUR PROGRAMMER YOU WANTED A PRINTOUT?

KNOCK KNOCKS! KNOCK KNOCKS! KNOCK KNOCKS! KNOCK KNOCKS!
CKS! KNOCK KNOCKS! KNOCK KNOCKS! KNOCK KNOCKS! KNOCK KNO
KNOCKS! KNOCK KNOCKS! KNOCK KNOCKS! KNOCK KNOCKS! KNOCK

KNOCK KNOCK!

WHO'S THERE?

ASCII.

ASCII WHO?

ASCII GOT A CODE IN HIS HEAD?

KNOCK KNOCKS! KNOCK KNOCKS! KNOCK KNOCKS! KNOCK KNOCKS!
CKS! KNOCK KNOCKS! KNOCK KNOCKS! KNOCK KNOCKS! KNOCK KNO
KNOCKS! KNOCK KNOCKS! KNOCK KNOCKS! KNOCK KNOCKS! KNOCK
NOCK KNOCKS! KNOCK KNOCKS! KNOCK KNOCKS! KNOCK KNOCKS! K
S! KNOCK KNOCKS! KNOCK KNOCKS! KNOCK KNOCKS! KNOCK KNOCK
NOCKS! KNOCK KNOCKS! KNOCK KNOCKS! KNOCK KNOCKS! KNOCK K
CK KNOCKS! KNOCK KNOCKS! KNOCK KNOCKS! KNOCK KNOCKS! KNO
KNOCK KNOCKS! KNOCK KNOCKS! KNOCK KNOCKS! KNOCK KNOCKS!

KNOCK KNOCKS!
KNOCK KNOCKS!
KNOCK KNOCKS!
KNOCK KNOCKS!
KNOCK KNOCKS!
KNOCK KNOCKS!
KNOCK KNOCKS!
KNOCK KNOCKS!
KNOCK KNOCKS!
KNOCK KNOCKS!
KNOCK KNOCKS!
KNOCK KNOCKS!
KNOCK KNOCKS!
KNOCK KNOCKS!
KNOCK KNOCKS!
KNOCK KNOCKS!
KNOCK KNOCKS!
KNOCK KNOCKS!
KNOCK KNOCKS!
KNOCK KNOCKS!
KNOCK KNOCKS!
KNOCK KNOCKS!
KNOCK KNOCKS!
KNOCK KNOCKS!
KNOCK KNOCKS!
KNOCK KNOCKS!
KNOCK KNOCKS!
KNOCK KNOCKS!
KNOCK KNOCKS!
KNOCK KNOCKS!
KNOCK KNOCKS!
KNOCK KNOCKS!
KNOCK KNOCKS!
KNOCK KNOCKS!
KNOCK KNOCKS!
KNOCK KNOCKS!

KNOCK KNOCK!
WHO'S THERE?
DISPLAY.
DISPLAY WHO?

DIS PLAY, DAT'S WORK.

KNOCK KNOCK!
WHO'S THERE?
DOS.
DOS WHO?

DOS DEBUG BYTE?

60 REM TOM SWIFT IN THE COMPUTER ROOM

"THE CRT IS OUT OF ORDER," TOM SAID DARKLY.

"I CAN'T FIND THE RIGHT FILE," TOM SAID DISKGUSTEDLY.

"MY PROGRAM HAS BLOWN UP," TOM CRIED EXPLOSIVELY.

"THIS COMPUTER HAS NO TUBES TO BLOW OUT," TOM STATED SOLIDLY.

65 REM BITS OF HISTORY

70 REM COMPUTERS AT PLAY

WHAT DO YOU CALL FOUR COMPUTERS THAT SING TOGETHER?

WHAT'S THEIR FAVORITE SONG?

A coretette.

"Sweet Apple-line."

HOW DO COMPUTERS MEET EACH OTHER?

HOW DO COMPUTERS SPEND SATURDAY NIGHTS?

DO COMPUTERS LIKE TO DANCE?

HOW DO THEY DANCE?

WHERE DO THEY GO DANCING?

Through computer dating services.

They go out on datas, of course.

Yes. They algorithm.

Chip to chip.

To a disk-o-tech.

WHAT'S A COMPUTER'S FAVORITE GAME?

WHAT'S A YOUNG COMPUTER'S FAVORITE GAME?

WHAT DO COMPUTERS DO FOR FUN?

WHAT'S THE BASIC PROBLEM WITH COMPUTERS?

Poker.

Peek-a-Boo or Hide-and-Go-Peek.

They stand around and give each other wrong answers.

They have a pretty dumb idea of fun.

WHERE DO COMPUTERS LIKE TO STROLL WHEN THEY HAVE A CLASS REUNION?

WHAT DO COMPUTERS YELL WHEN THEIR TEAM WINS?

Down memory lane.

"Hip, Hip, Array!"

WHAT'S THE NAME OF THE TV SERIES ABOUT AN ALIEN THAT BEFRIENDS AN EARTH COMPUTER?

WHAT DO YOU CALL MUSIC FROM A COMPUTER-OPERATED HORN?

WHAT'S THE NAME OF THE NEW HORROR MOVIE FOR COMPUTERS?

"Mork and Mini."

Out toot.

"Silent Screen."

WHAT DO YOU GET WHEN YOU CROSS A COMPUTER WITH A REFRIGERATOR?

WHAT DO YOU GET WHEN YOU CROSS A COMPUTER WITH A MIDGET?

WHAT DO YOU GET WHEN YOU CROSS A COMPUTER WITH A BLENDER?

WHAT DO YOU GET WHEN YOU CROSS A COMPUTER WITH AN ONION?

Very cool answers.

A short circuit.

A mixed solution.

Either a computer with a bad overflow problem, or answers that bring tears to your eyes.

WHAT DO YOU GET WHEN YOU CROSS A COMPUTER WITH AN ALLIGATOR?

WHAT DO YOU GET WHEN YOU CROSS A COMPUTER WITH AN ELEPHANT?

WHAT DO YOU GET WHEN YOU CROSS A COMPUTER WITH A RABBIT?

WHAT DO YOU GET WHEN YOU CROSS A COMPUTER WITH A PARROT?

WHAT DO YOU GET WHEN YOU CROSS A COMPUTER WITH A MULE?

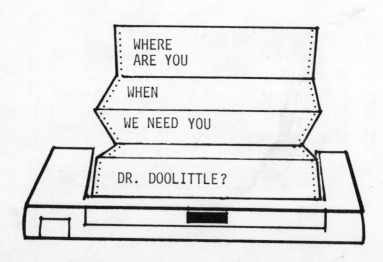

WHERE ARE YOU WHEN WE NEED YOU DR. DOOLITTLE?

Either snappy answers or a computer with a byte.

A five-ton know-it-all.

A computer that jumps to conclusions.

A computer that breaks down because its circuits are full of cracker crumbs.

A computer that gives you a real kick when you plug it in.

80 REM DAFFINITIONS

SILICON CHIP:	A boatful of criminals who don't know how to be serious.
SYNTAX ERROR:	A mistake on a burglar's income tax form.
KEYBOARD:	What you use to open the lock on your surfboard.

JOLLY ROBBERS

HA-HA

85 REM COMPUTERS TALKING TO COMPUTERS

WHAT DO COMPUTERS DO WHEN THEY MEET TO SOLVE A PROBLEM?

WHAT DID ONE COMPUTER SAY TO THE OTHER COMPUTER?

WHAT DID THE OTHER COMPUTER SAY BACK?

They have a diskussion.

"Whirrr, click-click, BEEP, BEEP, BEEP!"

"Whaddya mean, whirrr, click-click, BEEP, BEEP, BEEP?"

WHY DID THE MARRIED COMPUTERS GET A DIVORCE?

WHAT DID ONE SAY TO THE OTHER BEFORE THEY PARTED?

WHAT DID THE BIG COMPUTER CALL THE LITTLE COMPUTER?

WHAT DID THE LITTLE COMPUTER SAY TO THE BIG COMPUTER?

WHAT DID THE BIG COMPUTER SAY TO THE LITTLE COMPUTER?

They kept getting TYPE MISMATCH messages on their screens.

"You're rotten to the core!"

A chip off the old block.

"You're so disktinguished!"

"Power down, kid. You don't have enough chips for this game!"

WHAT DID THE PROUD MOTHER COMPUTER SAY TO HER SMART BABY?

WHAT DID THE DIGITAL CLOCK SAY TO ITS MOTHER?

"Data girl!"

"Look, Ma! No hands!"

90 REM KNOCK KNOCKS

KS! KNOCK KNOCKS! KNOCK KNOCKS! KNOCK KNOCKS! KNOCK KNO
KNOCKS! KNOCK KNOCKS! KNOCK KNOCKS! KNOCK KNOCKS! KNOCK
OCK KNOCKS! KNOCK KNOCKS! KNOCK KNOCKS! KNOCK KNOCKS! KN
! KNOCK KNOCKS! KNOCK KNOCKS! KNOCK KNOCKS! KNOCK KNOCKS
OCKS! KNOCK KNOCKS! KNOCK KN

KNOCK KNOCK!
WHO'S THERE?
CURSOR.
CURSOR WHO?

CURSOR GET AN ULCER!

KNOCK KNOCKS! KNOCK KNOCKS! KNOCK KNOCKS! KNOCK KNOCKS!
KS! KNOCK KNOCKS! KNOCK KNOCKS! KNOCK KNOCKS! KNOCK KNOC
KNOCKS! KNOCK KNOCKS! KNOCK KNOCKS! KNOCK KNOCKS! KNOCK

KNOCK KNOCK!
WHO'S THERE?
BYTE.
BYTE WHO?

BYTE UMINOUS COAL BURNS BEST.

! KNOCK KNOCKS! KNOCK KNOCKS! KNOCK KNOCKS! KNOCK KN
K KNOCKS! KNOCK KNOCKS! KNOCK KNOCKS! KNOCK KNOCKS! KNOC
KNOCK KNOCKS! KNOCK KNOCKS! KNOCK KNOCKS! KNOCK KNOCKS!
KS! KNOCK KNOCKS! KNOCK KNOCKS! KNOCK KNOCKS! KNOCK KNOC
KNOCKS! KNOCK KNOCKS! KNOCK KNOCKS! KNOCK KNOCKS! KNOCK
OCK KNOCKS! KNOCK KNOCKS! KNOCK KNOCKS! KNOCK KNOCKS! KN
! KNOCK KNOCKS! KNOCK KNOCKS! KNOCK KNOCKS! KNOCK KNOCKS
OCKS! KNOCK KNOCKS! KNOCK KNOCKS! KNOCK KNOCKS! KNOCK KN
K KNOCKS! KNOCK KNOCKS! KNOCK KNOCKS! KNOCK KNOCKS! KNO
KNOCK KNOCKS! KNOCK KNOCKS! KNOCK KNOCKS! KNOCK KNOCKS!

95 REM COMPUTERS IN THE CLASSROOM

WHAT'S THE DIFFERENCE BETWEEN A COMPUTER AND A CLASSROOM TEACHER?

WHY WON'T COMPUTERS EVER REPLACE CLASSROOM TEACHERS?

HOW IS A CLASSROOM COMPUTER LIKE A DENTIST?

Computers can't give dirty looks.
Computers can't give dirty looks.
They both use drills to fill gaps.

WHY DID THE COMPUTER GET THROWN OUT OF CLASS?

WHAT DID EVERYONE SAY WHEN THE SCIENCE TEACHER CROSSED A COMPUTER WITH A SKUNK?

WHY WON'T COMPUTERS EVER REPLACE BOOKS?

WHY WON'T COMPUTERS EVER REPLACE NEWSPAPERS?

For peeking and poking.

CPU!

There's no place to put the bookmark.

Have you ever tried to swat a fly with a computer?

DAFFINITIONS!

DUM-DE-DUM-DUM

100 REM DAFFINITIONS

ALGORITHM: Why Al is such a good drummer.

BUGS IN THE SYSTEM: Terminalites.

DATA: Something that brings two computers together on Saturday night.

KEYPUNCH: What keys drink at a party.

DISK DRIVE: A boulevard for UFOs.

MICROCOMPUTER: Not yourcrocomputer, or hiscro- or hercrocomputer either.

DISPLAY SCREEN: A play screen closer to you den dat play screen.

105 REM CONCATENATIONS

WHAT DO YOU CALL A COMPUTER DESIGNED FOR A CAT TO USE AT HOME?

WHAT DOES THE CAT GET FROM ITS PUSSONAL COMPUTER?

WHAT COMPUTER CAN BE USED BY EITHER A CAT OR A DOG?

A pussonal computer.

Meowput.

A pawsonal computer.

110 REM AND NOW FOR SOME CHIP LAUGHS

THERE ARE MANY COMPUTER DATING SERVICES THESE DAYS. WHAT'S THEIR PURPOSE?

WHAT DO THEY USE IN COMPUTERS IN IDAHO?

WHAT DO YOU CALL A ROBOT APE?

WHAT DO YOU CALL A MISER WHO AUTOMATES HIS ROLLER SKATES SO THAT HE WON'T HAVE TO BUY A CAR?

WHAT DO YOU CALL A MONASTERY RESIDENT WHO WORKS ON INTEGRATED CIRCUITS?

Friendchip and Courtchip.

Potato chips.

A chipanzee.

A chipskate.

A chipmonk.

115 REM COMPUTER CRIME

HOW DID THE COMPUTER MAKE A REAL KILLING?

WHY WAS THE COMPUTER ARRESTED?

WHERE DO THEY PUT A COMPUTER THAT COMMITS A CRIME?

WHAT DO YOU CALL A COMPUTER THAT GOES TO PRISON?

It executed the programmer.

For robbing the memory bank.

In the pokey, of course.

A conputer.

120 REM CHIPS AT SEA

WHAT DO YOU CALL AN AUTOMATED DINGHY?

WHAT KIND OF DISPLAY TERMINAL DO SAILORS USE?

WHAT DO YOU CALL A COMPLETELY AUTOMATED TUNA FLEET?

A robot rowboat.

A sea-R-T

Fishin' chips.

KNOCKS! KNOCK KNOCKS! KNOCK KNOCKS! KNOCK KNOCKS! KNOCK
OCK KNOCKS! KNOCK KNOCKS! KNOCK KNOCKS! KNOCK KNOCKS! KN
! KNOCK KNOCKS! KNOCK KNOCKS! KNOCK KNOCKS! KNOCK KNOCKS
OCKS! KNOCK KNOCKS! KNOCK KNOCKS! KNOCK KNOCKS! KNOCK KN
K KNOCKS! KNOCK KNOCKS! KNOCK KNOCKS! KNOCK KNOCKS! KNOC
KNOCK KNOCKS! KNOCK KNOCKS! KNOCK KNOCKS! KNOCK KNOCKS!
KS! KNOCK KNOCKS! KNOCK KNOCKS! KNOCK KNOCKS! KNOCK KNOC
KNOCKS! KNOCK KNOCKS! KNOCK KNOCKS! KNOCK KNOCKS! KNOCK
OCK KNOCKS! KNOCK KNOCKS! KNOCK KNOCKS! KNOCK KNOCKS! KN
KNOCKS! KNOCK KNOCKS! KNOCK KNOCKS! KNOCK KNOCKS! KNOCK
OCK KNOCKS! KNOCK KNOCKS! KNOCK KNOCKS! KNOCK KNOCKS! KN
KNOCK KNOCKS! KNOCK KNOCKS! KNOCK KNOCKS! KNOCK KNOCKS
OCKS! KNOCK KNOCKS! KNOCK KNOCKS! KNOCK KNOCKS! KNOCK KN
K KNOCKS! KNOCK KNOCKS! KNOCK KNOCKS! KNOCK KNOCKS! KNOC
KNOCK KNOCKS! KNOCK KNOCKS! KNOCK KNOCKS! KNOCK KNOCKS!
KS! KNOCK KNOCKS! KNOCK KNOCKS! KNOCK KNOCKS! KNOCK KNOC
KNOCKS! KNOCK KNOCKS! KNOCK KNOCKS! KNOCK KNOCKS! KNOCK
OCK KNOCKS! KNOCK KNOCKS! KNOCK KNOCKS! KNOCK KNOCKS! KN
KNOCK KNOCKS! KNOCK KNOCKS! KNOCK KNOCKS! KNOCK KNOCKS
OCKS! KNOCK KNOCKS! KNOCK KNOCKS! KNOCK KNOCKS! KNOCK KN
K KNOCKS! KNOCK KNOCKS! KNOCK KNOCKS! KNOCK KNOCKS! KNOC
KNOCK KNOCKS! KNOCK KNOCKS! KNOCK KNOCKS! KNOCK KNOCKS!
KS! KNOCK KNOCKS! KNOCK KNOCKS! KNOCK KNOCKS! KNOCK KNOC
KNOCKS! KNOCK KNOCKS! KNOCK KNOCKS! KNOCK KNOCKS! KNOCK
OCK KNOCKS! KNOCK KNOCKS! KNOCK KNOCKS! KNOCK KNOCKS! KN
KNOCK KNOCK KNOCKS! KNOCK KNOCKS! KNOCK KNOCKS
OCKS! KNOCK K KNOCKS! KNOCK KNOCKS! KNOCK KN
KNOCKS! KN KNOCKS! KNOCK KNOCKS! KNOC
KNOCK KNOCKS NOCK KNOCKS! KNOCK KNOCKS!
S! KNOCK KN S! KNOCK KNOCKS! KNOCK KNOC
KNOCKS! KNOC NOCKS! KNOCK KNOCKS! KNOCK
CK KNOCKS! K CK KNOCKS! KNOCK KNOCKS! KN
KNOCK KNOC KNOCK KNOCKS! KNOCK KNOCKS
CKS! KNOCK K CKS! KNOCK KNOCKS! KNOCK KN
KNOCKS! KN NOCK KNOCKS! KNOCK KNOCKS! KNOC
NOCK KNOCKS! KNOCK KNOCKS! KNOCK KNOCKS! KNOCK KNOCKS!
KS! KNOCK KNOCKS! KNOCK KNOCKS! KNOCK KNOCKS! KNOCK KNOC
NOCKS! KNOCK KNOCKS! KNOCK KNOCKS! KNOCK KNOCKS! KNOCK
CK KNOCKS! KNOCK KNOCKS! KNOCK KNOCKS! KNOCK KNOCKS! KN

CUTE AS
A BUG...
YECH!!

125 REM KNOCK KNOCKS

KNOCK KNOCK!
WHO'S THERE?
HARDWARE.
HARDWARE WHO?

HARD WHERE YOU RUN UP A HILL, EASY WHERE
YOU RUN DOWN.

KNOCK KNOCK!
WHO'S THERE?
BUG.
BUG WHO?

ANYONE BUG ME!

KNOCK KNOCK!
WHO'S THERE?
GOSUB.
GOSUB WHO?

HOLLYWOOD GOSUB, BY A GOSUB COLUMNIST.

IFTIES!   SWIFTIES!   SWIFTIES!   SWIFTIES!   SWIFTIES!   SWIFT
IFTIES!   SWIFTIES!   SWIFTIES!   SWIFTIES!   SWIFTIES!   SWIFT
IFTIES!   SWIFTIES!   SWIFTIES!   SWIFTIES!   SWIFTIES!   SWIFT
IFTIES!   SWIFTIES!   SWIFTIES!   SWIFTIES!   SWIFTIES!   SWIFT
IFTIES!   SWIFTIES!   SWIFTIES!   SWIFTIES!   SWIFTIES!   SWIFT
IFTIES!   SWIFTIES!   SWIFTIES!   SWIFTIES!   SWIFTIES!   SWIFT
IFTIES!   SWIFTIES!   SWIFTIES!   SWIFTIES!   SWIFTIES!   SWIFT
IFTIES!   SWIFTIES!   SWIFTIES!   SWIFTIES!   SWIFTIES!   SWIFT
IFTIES!   SWIFTIES!   SWIFTIES!   SWIFTIES!   SWIFTIES!   SWIFT
IFTIES!   SWIFTIES!   SWIFTIES!   SWIFTIES!   SWIFTIES!   SWIFT
IFTIES!   SWIFTIES!   SWIFTIES!   SWIFTIES!   SWIFTIES!   SWIFT
IFTIES!   SWIFTIES!   SWIFTIES!   SWIFTIES!   SWIFTIES!   SWIFT
IFTIES!   SWIFTIES!   SWIFTIES!   SWIFTIES!   SWIFTIES!   SWIFT
IFTIES!   SWIFTIES!   SWIFTIES!   SWIFTIES!   SWIFTIES!   SWIFT
IFTIES!   SWIFTIES!   SWIFTIES!   SWIFTIES!   SWIFTIES!   SWIFT
IFTIES!   SWIFTIES!   SWIFTIES!   SWIFTIES!   SWIFTIES!   SWIFT
IFTIES!   SWIFTIES!   SWIFTIES!   SWIFTIES!   SWIFTIES!   SWIFT
IFTIES!   SWIFTIES!   SWIFTIES!   SWIFTIES!   SWIFTIES!   SWIFT
IFTIES!   SWIFTIES!   SWIFTIES!   SWIFTIES!   SWIFTIES!   SWIFT
IFTIES!   SWIFTIES!   SWIFTIES!   SWIFTIES!   SWIFTIES!   SWIFT
IFTIES!   SWIFTIES!   SWIFTIES!   SWIFTIES!   SWIFTIES!   SWIFT
IFTIES!   SWIFTIES!   SWIFTIES!   SWIFTIES!   SWIFTIES!   SWIFT
IFTIES!   SWIFTIES!   SWIFTIES!   SWIFTIES!   SWIFTIES!   SWIFT
IFTIES!   SW   S!   SWIFTIES!   SWIFTIES!   SWIFT
IFTIES!   SW   S!   SWIFTIES!   SWIFTIES!   SWIFT
IFTIES!   SW   S!   SWIFTIES!   SWIFTIES!   SWIFT
IFTIES!   SW   S!   SWIFTIES!   SWIFTIES!   SWIFT
IFTIES!   SW   S!   SWIFTIES!   SWIFTIES!   SWIFT
IFTIES!   SW   S!   SWIFTIES!   SWIFTIES!   SWIFT
IFTIES!   SW   S!   SWIFTIES!   SWIFTIES!   SWIFT
IFTIES!   SW   HOT ZIGITY!   S!   SWIFTIES!   SWIFTIES!   SWIFT
IFTIES!   SWIFTIES!   SWIFTIES!   SWIFTIES!   SWIFTIES!   SWIFT
IFTIES!   SWIFTIES!   SWIFTIES!   SWIFTIES!   SWIFTIES!   SWIFT
IFTIES!   SWIFTIES!   SWIFTIES!   SWIFTIES!   SWIFTIES!   SWIFT
IFTIES!   SWIFTIES!   SWIFTIES!   SWIFTIES!   SWIFTIES!   SWIFT
IFTIES!   SWIFTIES!   SWIFTIES!   SWIFTIES!   SWIFTIES!   SWIFT

130 REM TOM SWIFT IN THE COMPUTER ROOM

"MY CPU WON'T GO ON," TOM SAID TERMINALLY.

"ALL OUR COMPUTERS ARE IN ONE ROOM,"
TOM SAID SYSTEMATICALLY.

"THE CHIPS ARE DOWN!" TOM CRIED BLANKLY.

"THE LOGIC OF THIS PROGRAM ESCAPES ME,"
TOM SAID UNTHINKINGLY.

"SOMEONE UNPLUGGED THIS COMPUTER,"
TOM SAID DISCONNECTEDLY.

"THE INTERSECTION OF THE SET OF GOOD COMPUTER
PROGRAMS AND THE PROGRAMS *YOU* WRITE IS THE
NULL SET," TOM SAID LOGICALLY.

"THIS PROGRAM IS VERY SIMPLE," TOM SAID BASICALLY.

"WATCH THAT CURSOR!" TOM SAID PROFANELY.

135 REM COMPUTER LITERACY OR ALL YOU NEED TO KNOW ABOUT THE HISTORY OF COMPUTERS

WHAT DO PASCAL, JACQUARD, AND HOLLERITH HAVE IN COMMON?

They're all dead.

140 REM YOUR FRIEND, THE COMPUTER...

WHAT'S THE DIFFERENCE BETWEEN A COMPUTER?

WHAT'S THE DIFFERENCE BETWEEN A COMPUTER?

Insufficient data   Does not compute

Ask me that again AND YOU'LL FIND OUT WHO'S IN CHARGE AROUND HERE!

END

SOME COMPUTER TERMS

This list may provide inspiration and stimulation for anyone who would like to contribute to the important new field of computer literacy introduced in this book. It may also reassure those who think that some of the jokes have no point.

algorithm	down
ASCII code	down time
BASIC	execute (the program)
bit	floppy disk
boot	for-next loop
boot up	FORTRAN
bug	gosub
byte	goto
calculate	hardware
calculator	input
catalog	insufficient data—does not compute
chip	keyboard
command	line
compatibility	line number
compute	list
computer	load
computerize	logic
core	loop
CPU (Central Processing Unit)	magnetic
CRT (Cathode Ray Tube)	memory
cursor	memory bank
data	menu
data bank	micro
data base	microcomputer
debug	minicomputer
digital	monitor
disk	nibble
diskette	on-line
display	off-line
display screen	output
DOS	PASCAL

A B C D E F G H I J K L

personal computer
poke and peek
power down
power up
print
printout
program
programmer
RAM (Random Access Memory)
read
read data
REM (remark)
return
ROM (Read-Only Memory)
run
save
software
statement
syntax error
system
terminal
transistor
type mismatch
up (boot up, power up, system is up)
volt

Microcomputers

APPLE
ATARI
PET
TI (Texas Instrument)
TRS

N O P Q R S T U V W X

ABOUT THE AUTHOR

ANN BISHOP has been a writer and editor, mostly in Language Arts and Reading, in various textbook publishing houses for many years. Currently an editor at Science Research Associates, she recently began a close and happy association with microcomputers—learning their language and their little ways, writing courseware for them, and writing guides to help teachers use and understand them. This book reflects aspects of computer sociology that have heretofore been unnoticed by other researchers in the field.

Mrs. Bishop lives in Chicago. This is her fifteenth riddle book.

ABOUT THE ILLUSTRATOR

JERRY WARSHAW has illustrated a number of children's books, including all of Ann Bishop's popular riddle books. He has written three books on how to draw and is a popular speaker with both children and adults. A Civil War buff, he designed the flag and seal for the State of Illinois' 150th birthday celebration, as well as the official emblem for the Illinois Constitutional Convention of 1970. Mr. Warshaw is a native Chicagoan, and he now makes his home in Evanston, Illinois, with his wife and daughter.